Tiny's BIG Adventure

BethAnn Snow

First Edition

NEWMAN SPRINGS PUBLISHING
320 Broad Street
Red Bank, NJ 07701

First originally published by Newman Springs Publishing 2020

ISBN 978-1-64801-513-7 (Paperback)
ISBN 978-1-64801-514-4 (Digital)

Printed in the United States of America

To my two tiny turtles, you are my greatest adventure

Tiny the Turtle was swimming along,
singing to himself a turtley song,
"I think I'll go find my friends and play.
Maybe we'll have an adventure today."

So Tiny the Turtle went swimming along,
singing to himself a turtley song,
“Charlie the Crab, come out and play.
We’re going on an adventure today.”

So Tiny and Charlie went swimming along,
singing to themselves a turtley song.
They picked up Sally the Shark along the way,
to join in their adventure today.

So Tiny the Turtle went swimming along,
singing to himself a turtley song,
with Charlie the Crab and Sally the Shark.
And they came to a cave that was very, *very* dark.

Tiny the Turtle stopped swimming along.
He stopped singing to himself a turtley song.
He huddled with Charlie the Crab and Sally the Shark,
looking at the cave that was oh so dark.
He stuttered, “W-w-ell, what are we
waiting for? Let’s go play.
We wanted to go on an adventure today.”

They moved together toward the dark cave,
acting like they were oh so brave.
They got to the entrance and took a peek in,
and all they could see was a big glistening fin.
Tiny and his friends got real scared and pale,
until they saw it was only Wally the Whale.

“Why, hello, friends,” Wally said with a grin.
“Welcome to my home. Would you like to come in?”
They had a great time, playing with their friends.
Tiny, Charlie, Sally, and Wally played until the day’s end.

When Tiny's mother tucked him in that night,
he told her about his day and how
Wally gave them a fright.
"Silly Tiny, that fear was all in your head."
Then she kissed him good night, and he went to bed.

The next day, Tiny the Turtle was swimming along,
singing to himself a turtley song,
"I think I'll go find my friends and play.
Perhaps we'll have another adventure today."

CPSIA information can be obtained
at www.ICGtesting.com
Printed in the USA
LVHW071349190122
708919LV00018B/839